STEP
THIS
WAY
FOR
AnOTHeR
GASkitts
StORY

First published 2002 by Walker Books Ltd
87 Vauxhall Walk, London SE11 5HJ

This edition published 2018

2 4 6 8 10 9 7 5 3 1

Text © 2002 Allan Ahlberg
Illustrations © 2002 Katharine McEwen

The right of Allan Ahlberg and Katharine McEwen to be identified
as author and illustrator respectively of this work has been asserted by them
in accordance with the Copyright, Designs and Patents Act 1988

This book has been typeset in Stempel Schneidler,
Cafeteria, Tapioca and Kosmik

Printed in China

British Library Cataloguing in Publication Data:
a catalogue record for this book
is available from the British Library

ISBN 978-1-4063-8165-8

www.walker.co.uk

MIAOW!

Contents

Meet The Gaskitts

(and Horace's friend)

Mrs Gaskitt

A taxi-driver and loving mother who likes to enter competitions.

Mr Gaskitt

A fond hard-working father who always takes any job he can get.

Gus and Gloria Gaskitt

Nine-and-a-half-year-old twins.

Horace Gaskitt

A ginger-and-white cat
who likes to argue
with his friend.

No, I don't!
Yes, you do!
No, I don't!
Yes, you do!
No, I...
Yes, you...
No...
Yes...

Horace's Friend

A black cat
who likes to argue
with Horace.

The Gaskitts' Doormat

Mostly welcoming...

LOVELY TO
SEE YOU!

Sometimes grumpy...

WIPE YOUR
FEET!

Sometimes rude...

BEAT IT!

Chapter One
Mrs Gaskitt's Luck Begins

One morning in the month of May

Mrs Gaskitt got up.

Good morning, Mrs Gaskitt!

She came downstairs, gave Horace a bowl

of Crunchy Mice

and gave his

friend one too.

He was there

on a visit.

Thanks,
Mrs Gaskitt!

Mrs Gaskitt got

Gus and Gloria up,

gave *them* their breakfasts

and sent them off to school.

She read the paper,

drank a cup of tea,

picked up the post

as it came tumbling

through the letterbox,

opened the door ...

and kissed the

postman!

But what about *Mr* Gaskitt?

Never mind –

he *was* the postman.

It was his latest job.

Meanwhile, Gus and Gloria were in the playground

watching – Oh no! – their poor teacher, Mrs Fritter,

falling off her bike at the school gates.

Mrs Fritter hit the pavement

with a terrible bang,

got some nasty cuts and bruises

on her arms and legs, and had to go home.

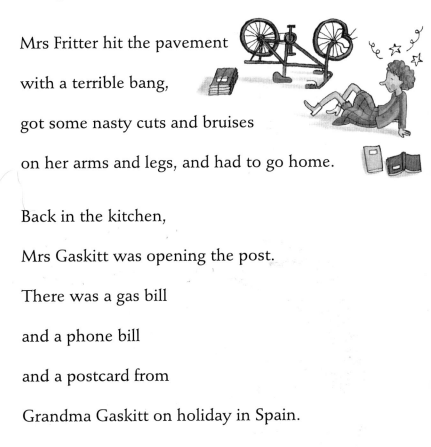

Back in the kitchen,

Mrs Gaskitt was opening the post.

There was a gas bill

and a phone bill

and a postcard from

Grandma Gaskitt on holiday in Spain.

There was a vet's appointment for Horace …

and one more envelope.

Mrs Gaskitt opened it.

Congratulations!

Congratulations, Mrs Gaskitt!

said the letter.

You have won first prize in our

most amazing competition.

"Wow!" cried Mrs Gaskitt.

"This must be my lucky day."

Chapter Two
One Little Question

Half an hour later, a van

stopped outside the Gaskitts' house.

It had Mrs Gaskitt's prize in it:

A YEAR'S SUPPLY OF

CRUNCHY MICE.

"All I did was answer

one little question," said Mrs Gaskitt.

"Fancy that," said the van man.

"And make up one little caption."

CRUNCHY
MICE ARE
TWICE AS NICE!

"This must be your lucky

day," the van man said.

Mrs Gaskitt's prize filled the kitchen.

Horace's friend was amazed.

So was the doormat.

So was Horace.

"This must be

my lucky day,"

he thought.

WOW!

Back at the school, a supply teacher

had arrived in Gus and Gloria's classroom.

This supply teacher was

rather short

and rather wide.

She had silvery hair,

dangly earrings,

a big smile ...

"Hello, dearies!"

... and a huge suitcase.

On wheels.

"My name," she said, "is Mrs Plum."

And she *opened the case*.

Meanwhile, back in the kitchen,

Horace and his friend were purring loudly and gazing

up at the piles and piles

of Crunchy Mice.

The word had spread.

Horace's other friends were

at the window, peeping in.

"I bet that lot would

last me ... a year!"

cried Horace.

"Well, it would," said his friend.

"It's a year's supply."

"Oh, yeah," said Horace.

"Or half a year's supply

for two cats," said his friend.

"Yeah," said Horace.

"Or a month's supply

for twelve cats."

"Yeah!"

"Or a day's supply

for three hundred and sixty-five cats!"

"YEAH!"

"Or a *party*," miaowed Horace's friends

from outside. "For us."

Chapter Three
Mrs Plum's Suitcase

Mrs Plum took out of her suitcase:

a ball of wool and some knitting

a photograph in a silver frame

a vase of flowers (plastic)

a small guitar

a sandwich maker

a pair of pink fluffy slippers

and a box of

chocolates.

There was silence in the room.

The children gazed in wonder

at Mrs Plum,

the knitting,

the sandwich maker

and the chocolates.

"This must be *our* lucky

day," they thought.

Mrs Plum put the flowers

and the photograph on

her desk,

and the slippers on her feet.

She opened the box of chocolates

and popped one into her mouth.

"Now then, dearies, let's get started."

The day went by in Mrs Plum's class and the children loved it. They had cooking lessons with the sandwich maker, science lessons *fixing* the sandwich maker and singing lessons with the guitar.

Mrs Plum read stories to them, gave them some easy sums and shared her chocolates. When the box was empty, she opened her suitcase and took out another.

21

By the end of the day

the children could not believe their luck.

Mrs Plum was the best teacher they had ever had.

The best in the school,

in the town,

in the universe!

Yes, everything was perfect.

Well, *almost* everything.

The only trouble was

that in all the excitement

a few little things ...

had gone missing.

Billy Turpin had lost his football boots.

Tracey Appledrop had lost her pencil case.

Gloria Gaskitt had lost her lucky charm bracelet.

But even then Mrs Plum

was *so* kind

    so helpful

    so sympathetic.

She looked everywhere

in that classroom,

searched high and low,

but with no luck at all.

When home-time came,

the missing things were still missing.

Chapter Four
Mrs Gaskitt's Luck Continues

Two days later, Mrs Gaskitt got up again.

Of course, she got up on the day in between

as well, but nothing happened then.

Yes ...

Mrs Gaskitt got up,

Good morning,
Mrs Gaskitt!

fed the children,

fed the cats,

Thanks,
Mrs Gaskitt!

read the paper,

drank the tea,

heard a familiar sound

out in the street

– Clink, clink! –

opened the door,

picked up the milk ...

and kissed the milkman!

But what about *Mr* Gaskitt?

Never mind –

he *was* the milkman.

It was his very latest job.

Meanwhile – Oh no! – poor Mrs Fritter

was falling over in the doctor's waiting room.

The doctor had just said

she was well enough to return to work.

Now Mrs Fritter had more cuts and bruises

and needed to go back to bed again.

Meanwhile, Mrs Plum was fit and well.

She played football with the boys,

and netball with the girls.

Shoot, dearie!

At playtime, Mrs Plum

drank tea in the staffroom

with the other teachers.

More sugar,
Mr Blagg?

The other teachers liked Mrs Plum.

She told them funny stories

about her long life as a teacher,

shared her chocolates,

and helped them to look for things ...

when they

went missing.

Where's my
umbrella?

Who's seen
my mobile
phone?

27

Back at the Gaskitts' house,

the phone was ringing.

Mrs Gaskitt was outside washing her taxi.

In she ran and picked up the receiver.

"Congratulations, Mrs Gaskitt!"

said a man on the phone.

"You have won first prize in our—"

"Wow!" cried Mrs Gaskitt.

"*Another* lucky day."

Chapter Five
One Little Coupon

Two hours later, a lorry

"BEEP, BEEP, I AM REVERSING!"

stopped outside the Gaskitts'

house. It had Mrs Gaskitt's

prize in it:

A COMPLETE HOUSEFUL OF FURNITURE!

"All I did was fill in one little coupon,"

said Mrs Gaskitt.

"Well, I never," said the driver.

"And put some ticks in boxes."

"BEEP, BEEP, I AM AMAZED!"

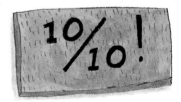

Mrs Gaskitt's prize filled every room in the house

(and the kitchen twice over).

Horace and his friend went round sitting on things.

They were amazed too.

"She's very lucky, my Mrs," said Horace.

"I wonder why."

"Perhaps she's got a lucky horseshoe,"

said his friend. "Or a rabbit's foot –

or a four-leaf clover."

"Or a ten-leaf clover," said Horace.

"There's no such thing," said his friend.

"Yes, there is."

"No, there isn't."

"Yes, there is."

Yes, there is.

31

Meanwhile, back at the school,

it was almost home-time.

Some of the children had their coats on,

some were lined up by the door

and some ...

were looking for things.

Gus and Gloria were giving Randolph, the class rat,

some clean water and a slice of carrot.

"Now then, dearies," said Mrs Plum.

"Before you go – a message.

I'm planning a little trip soon—"

"Hooray!"

"Great, Miss!"

"I love a trip!"

"Where to, Miss?"

"Where we going?"

"Er ... somewhere nice," said Mrs Plum.

"A sort of mystery tour."

"Brilliant!"

"A mystery tour!"

"I love a mystery tour!"

"I've been on one before!"

"I've been on two!"

"Bring £10," Mrs Plum said.

"Tomorrow, if you can."

"I can bring £10, Miss!"

"I can bring twenty!"

"A hundred!"

As the children hurried off,

Mrs Plum called after them.

"One last thing – make it *cash*, dearies."

She popped a chocolate into

Billy Turpin's mouth.

"No cheques."

Chapter Six
Two Thousand Pounds!

The next day Mrs Gaskitt won:

a holiday for four

a caravan

a free hairdo

and a packet

of Protts!!

She told her family

and her friends

and her cat all about it.

"All I did was..."

Horace was pleased, of course,

and proud of Mrs Gaskitt.

But he was puzzled too.

"A holiday for *four* – what use is that?

Should be a holiday for five."

"Or six," said his friend.

"Or eleven," said his other friends

outside the window.

Meanwhile, Mrs Plum had collected

twenty-seven £10 notes from

the children and put them

in a safe place.

On wheels.

The children were excited about the trip,

and excited also about the school fete,

only a day away.

Mr Blagg, the headmaster, made a

little speech about it to the whole school.

There would be book stalls and cake stalls,

raffles and hoop-las, a coconut-shy and

a fancy dress competition.

There'd be a pet show (with prizes),

maypole dancing,

five-a-side for the dads

and an egg-and-spoon race

for the mums.

"Last year, children – Sh!" said Mr Blagg,

"– we raised £1,943.78p for the school fund."

"Hooray!" the children yelled.

"Sh!" said Mr Blagg.

"So this time, let's break the record.

Let's make it – Sh!

– two thousand pounds!"

"Hooray!" "Hooray!" the children yelled again.

Just then, up jumped Mrs Plum.

She couldn't stop herself.

"Two thousand pounds!" she cried,

and her big smile filled the hall.

"I'll help!"

Chapter Seven
Some Funny Business

At lunchtime, Mrs Gaskitt

ate her free packet of Protts

and had her free hairdo.

Lucky Mrs Gaskitt.

Meanwhile – Oh no!

– *un*lucky Mrs Fritter.

Mrs Fritter had just popped

into the chemist's for some

painkillers and a bandage.

On her way home and outside the *Travel Agent's*,

she was knocked flying by a short, wide lady

with charming manners,

"Beg pardon, dearie!"

and a huge suitcase.

On wheels.

The lady, however,

was very apologetic and *very* kind.

She helped Mrs Fritter to her feet

and gave her a chocolate.

Later that afternoon,

Gus and Billy Turpin were in the classroom

giving Randolph some exercise.

Gloria and Tracey Appledrop were painting a sign

for the Guess the Weight of the Cake competition.

Just then a phone rang.

"A phone, Miss! A phone!"

"Who's ringing us?"

"Where is it?"

Well, would you believe it, the phone was

ringing from *inside* Mrs Plum's suitcase.

"It's playing a tune, Miss!"

"So it is, dearie," said Mrs Plum,

and she gave the suitcase a kick.

"I know that tune, Miss!"

"Me too!"

"It's the same as

Mr Blagg's phone!"

"Yeah!"

"Only he's *lost* his!"

"So he has, dearie," said Mrs Plum

and she gave the case another kick.

"I helped him look for it."

Meanwhile, Gus and Gloria and some of the

other children were exchanging glances.

There was some funny business here.

Why did Mrs Plum not open the case?

Come to think of it, why did she *never* open it

(apart from that first morning)?

All of a sudden,

the whole class became suspicious.

They smelled a rat, all right ...

and it was *not* Randolph.

Chapter Eight
Handsome Horace

The next day,

which was a Saturday,

Mrs Gaskitt leapt out of bed,

raced downstairs,

flew into the

crowded kitchen:

2 tables

8 chairs

25 cartons of Crunchy Mice,

Good morning, Mrs...

fed the children,

fed Horace,

Thanks, Mrs...

read the paper,

read the post,

opened the back door,

kissed the milkman ...

Thanks, Mrs...

and went red in the face.

It was the *wrong* milkman.

50

Meanwhile, Gus and Gloria

were grooming Horace.

They brushed his coat till it shone,

tied a new pink ribbon around his neck

and told him how handsome he was.

Horace purred with pride.

He wished his friend was there to see him.

Later that morning,

Mrs Gaskitt was

still rushing around –

finding her trainers,

boiling an egg –

while Gus and Gloria

followed her about and

tried to get her attention.

"It's that supply teacher, Mum."

"Hm." Mrs Gaskitt was cooling her egg.

"The one with the suitcase."

"Yes." Mrs Gaskitt was

putting her trainers on.

"Which she *never* opens!"

"Ah." Mrs Gaskitt was

getting a spoon from

the cutlery drawer.

"Well, *we* think ..."

Mrs Gaskitt was out

through the door,

"... she's definitely ..."

into the garden

and off down the path

with her egg and spoon.

"... up to something!"

53

Chapter Nine
Mrs Plum Lends a Hand

It was a warm May afternoon.

The school fete was in full swing.

The grand total is now £100!

The maypole dancers were dancing

and delicious smells:

ice-cream

candy-floss

hot dogs

filled the air.

54

The grand total is now £200!

Mums and dads were working hard.

The infants were rushing

around in their

fancy dress

costumes.

Grand total £250!

Horace, with his beautiful ribbon,

was lined up with the other pets

in the pet show.

And the money... *£300!*

...was

pouring

in.

Meanwhile, Mrs Gaskitt was winning things.

She guessed the weight of the cake,

"All I did was..."

and the number of sweets in a jar.

She won a teddy,

a bottle of wine,

three goldfish,

five kilograms of grass seed

and a lawnmower.

And Horace saw ... most of it.

He purred with pride.

£500! - - - - -

"I know her," he told a guinea pig.

"Oh yes." The guinea pig was not

interested in Mrs Gaskitt.

He had other worries.

"Do I look stupid in this bow?"

"No," said Horace. "Not really."

The guinea pig scowled. "Hm. Bet I do."

MAURICE.   HORACE.   RON.

But, of course, what (you will be

wanting to know),

what about Mrs Plum?

Well, Mrs Plum was here,

there and everywhere.

She helped with

the refreshments.

Where's my...?

Where's...?

She helped with the fancy dress.

She helped with the coconut shy.

...?

The children – Gus and Gloria,

Tracey, Billy and the others – followed

Mrs Plum and watched her like hawks.

But the crowds were so big, the noise so loud,

the delicious smells so ... delicious,

that the children didn't *always* see

what she was up to.

Meanwhile, Mr Blagg ...

£1,200!

was looking happier,

£1,300!

and happier,

£1,500!

and happier.

£1,750!

Horace's new friend was looking happier too.

He had just won a rosette.

"So what's your name then?" he asked.

"Horace," said Horace.

"Fancy that – mine's Maurice. Horace and Maurice!"

"Yeah," said Horace, "all we need is a Boris."

"Or a Doris," said Maurice.

"Or a ... Poris," said Horace.

"*Poris?* There's no such name."

"Yes, there is," said Horace.

"No, there isn't."

Yes, there is.

Now, Mrs Gaskitt

and the other mothers were lining up ...

£1,900!

for the egg-and-spoon race.

£1,999.99!

Mr Blagg

jumped on his chair.

"We've made it –

Sh!" he yelled.

"Grand total –

two thousand

pounds!"

"Hooray!" "Hooray!"

The crowd cheered, then cheered again

as the egg-and-spoon race began.

It was a tremendous contest.

First Mrs Turpin was in the lead,

then she dropped her egg.

Then Mrs Appledrop was in the lead

and she dropped her egg.

Then Mrs Gaskitt

was in the lead and...

Meanwhile, all eyes (except two)

were on the race.

The children were watching (and yelling).

Horace was watching (and purring with pride).

Even Mr Blagg on his chair

was watching.

All of a sudden, Mr Blagg

looked down at the table and

was *not* happy any more.

The cash box,

the two thousand pounds,

even Mr Blagg's favourite pencil

(which his dear old mother

had given him) ...

had disappeared.

Oh no –
Grand total –
£nil!

Chapter Ten
Oops!

Now, of course, there was uproar at the
school fete. Everyone was yelling and
rushing around.

Well, nearly everyone.

Meanwhile, the egg-and-spoon race
was still in progress.
Mrs Gaskitt
got up speed,
while her egg, luckily,
stayed on its spoon.
She ran like the wind,
broke the tape, won the race, and –

Oh no! – *collided* with a short, wide lady,

silvery hair,

big smile,

suitcase (on wheels)

and knocked her flying.

Knocked her

suitcase flying too,

which rolled

and bounced

and rolled again ...

and burst open.

The crowd was astonished...

And all that Mrs Plum,

as she sat on the grass

with an egg in her lap,

could think to say was...

Later, when the police arrived, Mrs Plum had rather more to say.

"Can't think what came over me, dearies."

She smiled at Mr Blagg.

"Never done anything like this before."

"Yes, you have," said the inspector. "Loads of times."

"She's a very clever woman," the inspector explained.

"Thank you, dearie!"

"Robbed more schools than I've had hot dinners. Been on her trail for ages."

The inspector shook hands with Mr Blagg and congratulated Mrs Gaskitt on her lucky collision. "This should put a stop to Mrs Plum (alias Mrs Peach, alias Mrs Pomegranate) and her little games for a while, I shouldn't wonder." He climbed into his police car.

Hm. Where's my whistle?

Chapter Eleven
Mrs Gaskitt's Luck Runs Out

It was a warm May evening.

Mrs Gaskitt walked home

Good evening, Mrs Gaskitt!

with her children,

her cat and her prizes.

Gus and Gloria were telling

their mum all about Mrs Plum.

Mum, Plum – that rhymes!

Mrs Gaskitt was telling

Gus and Gloria

(and Horace)

how she had won

the teddy,

the bottle of wine

and all the other things.

"All I did..."

Suddenly, not looking

where she was going,

Mrs Gaskitt walked

straight under a

window cleaner's ladder.

Oh no! – *un*lucky Mrs Gaskitt.

Water from the window
cleaner's bucket
came splashing down and
soaked her to the skin.

And that wasn't the end of it.

Next thing, would you believe it,

the *window cleaner himself*

came scrambling down,

grabbed Mrs Gaskitt,

hauled her to her feet –

and kissed her!

But what about *Mr* Gaskitt?

Well, you've guessed it,

haven't you?

Yes – it was

his latest job.

Meanwhile, Horace was thinking hard ...

about luck.

"Hm. Lucky rabbit's foot – no.

Lucky horseshoes – no.

Lucky four-leaf clovers – no.

Lucky black cats..."

It was a warm May night.

The Gaskitts were asleep

in their crowded bedrooms.

The goldfish were getting

used to their new home.

The garage was full of grass seed.

Horace and his friend were

downstairs playing cards.

"It's you!" said Horace.

"What is?" said his friend. "SNAP! – I win."

"That's it – you always win!" said Horace.

"You're the *lucky black cat*!"

"No, I'm not – SNAP!" said his friend.

"Yes, you are."

"No, I'm not."

"Yes, you are."

"No, I'm not."

"Yes, you are."

"No, I'm ... not!"

"Yes ... you ... *yawn* ... are."

79

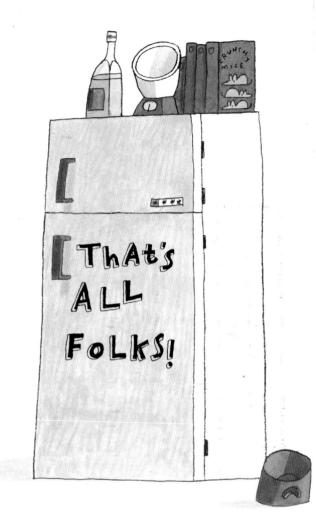

That's
ALL
Folks!

THE END